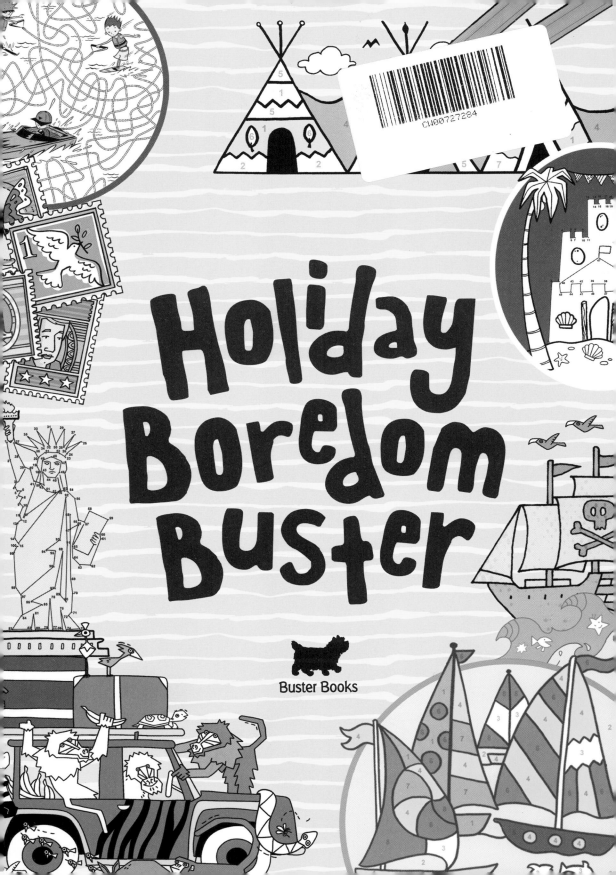

Holiday Boredom Buster

Buster Books

WRITTEN BY ELLEN BAILEY AND GUY CAMPBELL
ILLUSTRATED BY ADRIAN BARCLAY, EMILY GOLDEN TWOMEY,
CLIVE GOODYER, LISA JACKSON, PAUL MORAN,
ANDY ROWLAND, NELLIE RYAN
AND DANIEL SANCHAZ

EDITED BY HELEN BROWN, HANNAH COHEN,
JONNY MARX, SALLY PILKINGTON AND JEN WAINWRIGHT
DESIGNED BY JANENE SPENCER, DERRIAN BRADDER,
ZOE BRADLEY AND JACK CLUCAS
COVER DESIGN BY ANGIE ALLISON

This edition first published in Great Britain in 2018 by Buster Books,
an imprint of Michael O'Mara Books Limited, 9 Lion Yard, Tremadoc Road, London SW4 7NQ

 www.mombooks.com/buster Buster Books @BusterBooks

The material in this book previously appeared in *Buster's Brilliant Dot to Dot*,
Buster's Brilliant Colour by Numbers, *Colossal City Count*, *Colossal Creature Count*, *Dot to Dot*,
Ocean Doodles, *The Boys' Holiday Book*, *The Boys' Summer Book*, *The Girls' Holiday Book*,
The Girls' Summer Book, *Travel Doodles*.

Mazes generated by www.mazegenerator.net

ISBN: 978-1-78055-568-3

3 5 7 9 10 8 6 4

This book was printed in December 2018 by Gutenberg Press Ltd,
Gudja Road, Tarxien GXQ 2902, Malta.

HOW TO USE
THIS BOOK

This book is bursting with boredom-busting holiday fun.
All you need are your pens and pencils to enjoy
fill-in games, solve puzzles, colour pictures,
join dots and do your own doodles.

Follow the instructions on each page and check all
your answers at the back of the book.

What are you waiting for?
Dive right in!

AHOY THERE!

Test your seafaring strategy skills
with these boat-tastic brainteasers.

OH BUOY!

All the boats are coming back to the harbour
and you are the harbour master. Each buoy must have
at least one boat horizontally or vertically next to it.

The numbers tell you how many boats
there can be in each row or column.

Can you make sure each buoy has a boat?

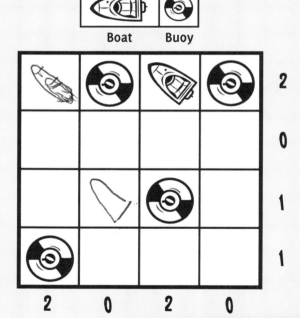

BATTLESHIP BRAINTEASER

There are a total of three cruisers, three launches and three buoys in this grid. Two buoys, two cruisers and a launch have been revealed for you. Can you find the rest?

The numbers tell you how many squares or groups of occupied squares there are in each row or column.

For example the numbers '4, 2' tell you there is a group of four squares together and a group of two squares together, with at least one empty square between them.

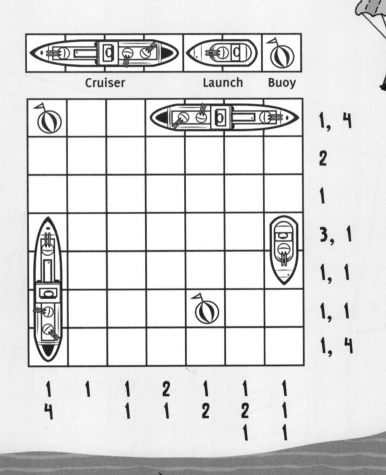

TREASURE

Colour the chest and fill it with treasures.

Add more islands and details to this treasure map.

HAPPY HERD

Join the dots to reveal a BIG picture.

SECRET SAFARI

You're visiting a safari park,
but where are all the animals?

Below is a map of the safari park.
To read it you will need to use coordinates.
A coordinate is a letter and a number that refers to a location
on a map. To use a coordinate, place your finger on the letter
on the left-hand side of the map. Trace your finger along the
row to the column that matches the number. In that square
you will find the animal that the coordinate refers to.

Can you work out which animals live at the following
coordinates?

1. D3 **2.** B1 **3.** F3 **4.** C6 **5.** A4 **6.** E6

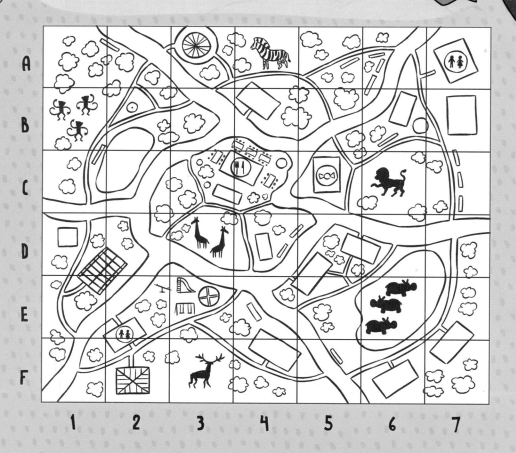

FIND THE MISSING NUMBER

Each animal in this grid represents
a number – either 1, 2, 3 or 4.

If you add up the numbers in any row or column,
you get the total at the end of that row or column.

For example, three elephants and a tiger equals 5,
and two elephants, a tiger and a lion equals 8.

Work out which animal represents which number,
and then work out the missing number.

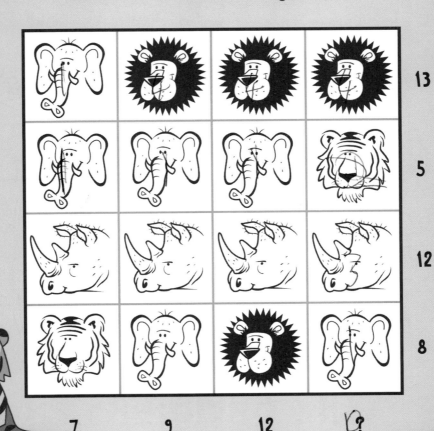

COLOUR IN
THE SAVANNA

GRAND SANDCASTLE

Follow the numbers to reveal a magnificent sandcastle.

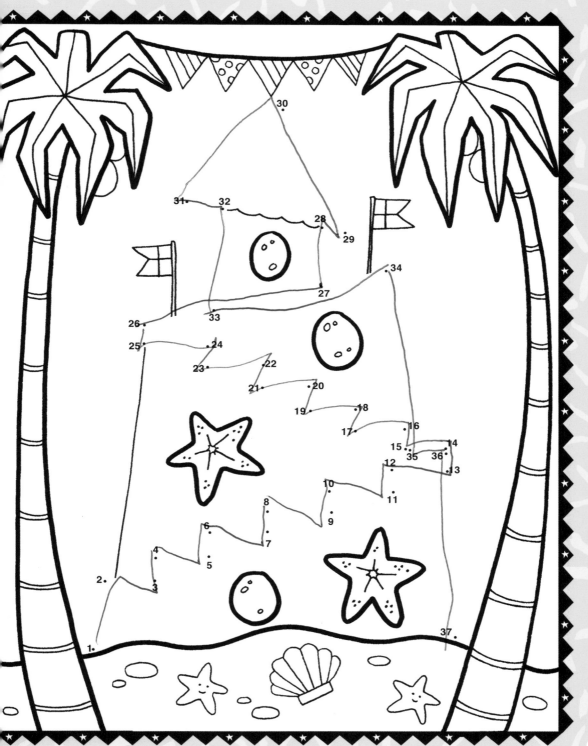

PICTURE PUZZLER

Tackle these picture puzzles. The first one is a brain-teaser, the second one is a brain-buster!

Complete this grid so that the four different pictures shown below appear in every row, in every column, and in each outlined block of four squares.

FANCY A HARDER PUZZLE?

Have a go at completing the grid below so the nine different pictures shown at the bottom of the page appear in every row, every column and in each outlined block of nine squares.

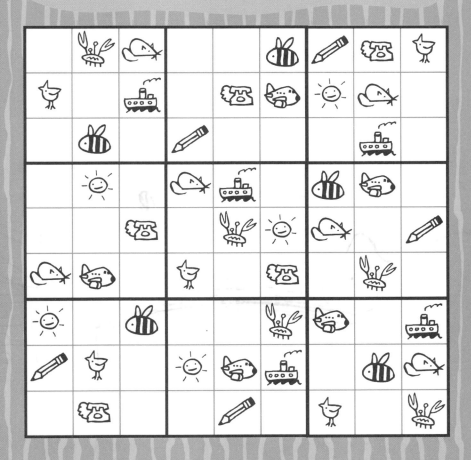

Decorate and colour
the turtle's shell.

BE A LOCAL

Learn to say, 'Hello, how are you?', 'It's really hot' and 'Where is the beach?' in six different languages. A guide to how to pronounce the words is given in *italics* below.

FRENCH

Bonjour, comment ça va?
Bonjhoor, common sa va?

Il fait très chaud!
Eel fay tray show!

Où est la plage?
Ooh ai la plahj?

GERMAN

Hallo! Wie geht's?
Ha-llo, vee gates?

Es ist sehr heiß!
Ess ist zair heiss!

Wo ist der Strand?
Vo ist dair shtrant?

SPANISH

¡Hola! Qué tal?
Oh-lah, kay tal?

Hace mucho calor!
Athay moochoh calaw!

Donde esta la playa?
Donday estah la plyah?

PORTUGUESE

Olá! Tudo bem?
Oh-lah! Toodoh baym?

Faz muito calor!
Fazjh mweetu cahlaw!

Onde é a praia?
On-duh ay ah prajah?

RUSSIAN

Privet, kak ti?
Preevyet, kak tiy?

Oi, kak zharko.
Oi, kak zharrko.

A gde plyazh?
A gd-yay plyazh?

ITALIAN

Ciao! Come stai?
Chow! Comeh stye?

Fa molto caldo!
Fa molto caaldo!

Dov'e' la spiaggia?
Doh-veh la spee-a-gee-ah?

GONE FISHING

Complete the maze to take the anchor to the bottom of the sea.

TREASURE HUNT

Blackbeard's treasure map has been found.

Blackbeard has buried two cutlasses, two amulets, two keys and two bars of Spanish silver, and their location is shown in this grid map. He forgot to mark where the cutlasses are and where he has hidden the missing key. Can you find them in the grid map below?

HOW TO PLAY

1. The numbers beside each row and under each column tell you how many squares in that row or that column are occupied.

For example, the top row has the numbers 1 and 2 by it, which tells you that 3 squares are occupied – one square on its own and then two squares right next to each other.

2. You can see where the two amulets are, both bars of silver and one of the keys that have been buried. Can you work out where the two cutlasses and the missing key are hidden?

Top Tip: Start by putting an 'X' in squares that you know are occupied, and an 'O' in squares you know are empty. When you have an 'X' or an 'O' in each of the squares, you should be able to work out what lies buried beneath them.

THE TREASURE

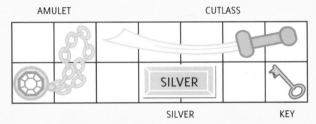

THE GRID MAP

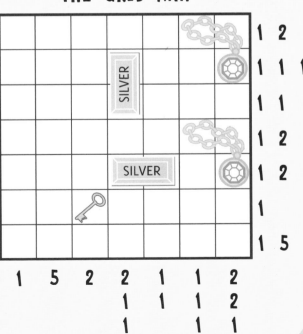

MASTER BUILDER

Below is a picture of the Taj Mahal, a beautiful building in India. Every year, millions of tourists flock to admire it. Using the squares in the grid below to help you, can you copy it?

Add more rows of waves in different colours.

SPOT THE DIFFERENCE

Can you find the 6 differences between these two scenes?

THINGS THAT GO

Kick-start your brain into gear
with these fun puzzles.

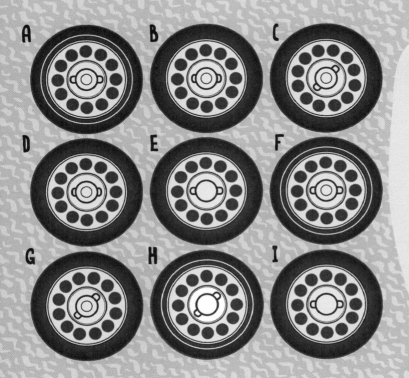

WHICH WHEELS?

These nine wheels look very similar, but in fact there are four matching pairs and one wheel that is not like any other.

Can you pick out the four pairs and spot the wheel that is the odd one out?

BITS 'N' PIECES

Only one of the boxes below contains all the bits needed to make this picture of a plane. Can you work out which box it is?

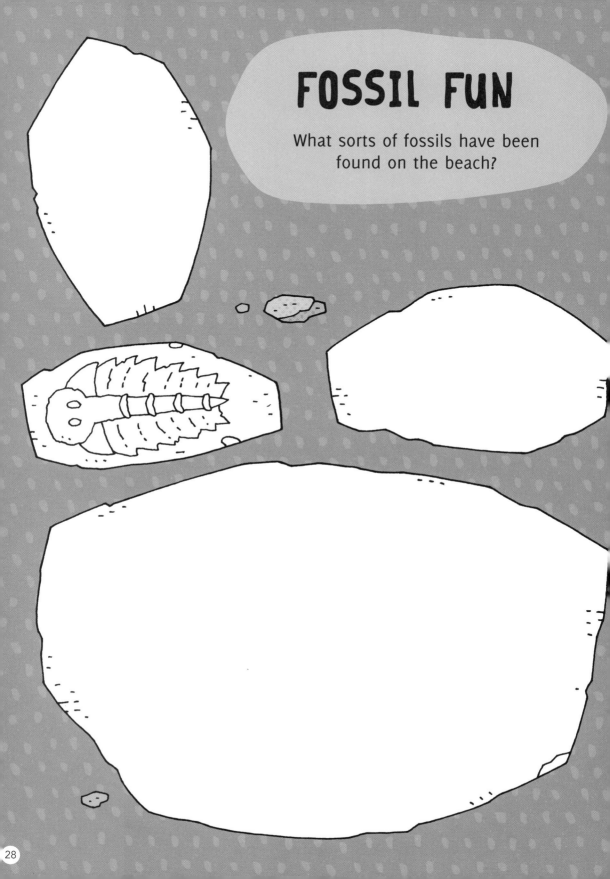

FOSSIL FUN

What sorts of fossils have been found on the beach?

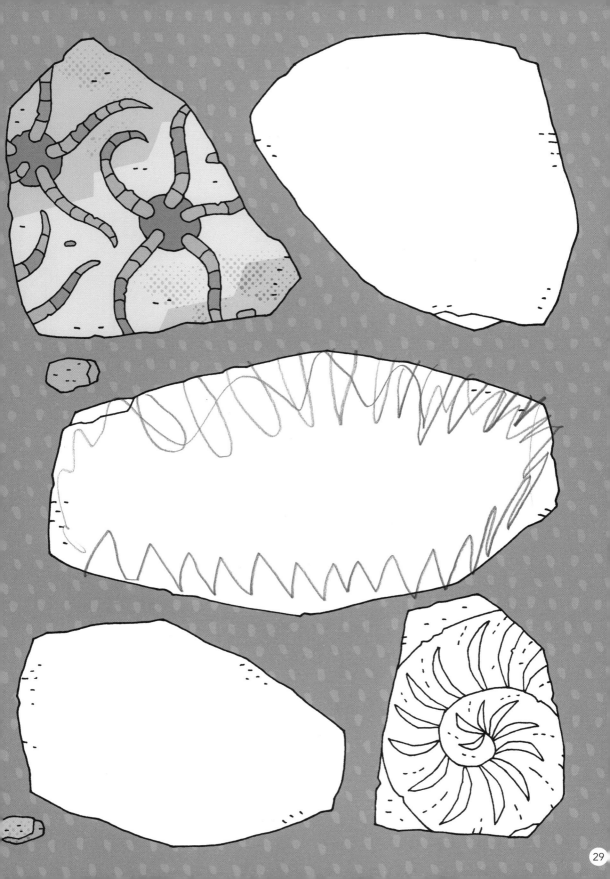

MAP MAYHEM

In map reading, combinations of letters and numbers are known as coordinates and refer to locations on the map. To use a coordinate, place your finger on the number given. Trace your finger along the row to the column that matches the letter. In that square you will find the symbol that the coordinates refer to.

1. 5A　　**2.** 4E　　**3.** 1F　　**4.** 3B　　**5.** 6D　　**6.** 3G

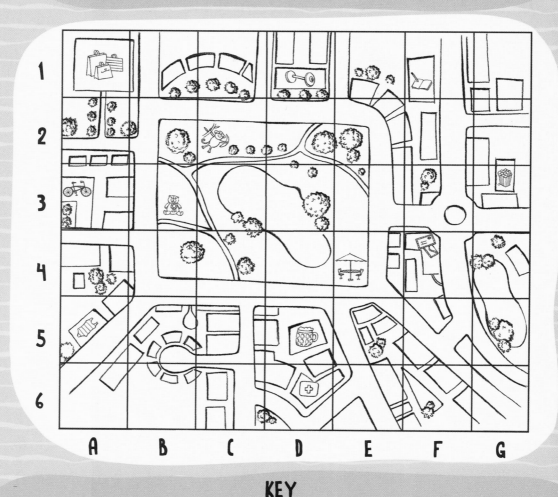

KEY

 pub　　 gym　　 hospital　　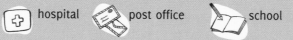 post office　　school　　 swimming pool

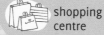 shopping centre　　 zoo　　 café　　 theme park　　 bike hire　　 cinema

ISLAND DISCOVERY

Test your map-reading skills by studying the map below. Can you answer the questions using the compass above to help you?

1. What number is on the sailing boat to the northeast of the island?

2. How many round huts are located in the northwest of the island?

3. Is the giant head positioned in the east or west of the island?

4. What tall building is at the island's most southwesterly point?

5. What is immediately east of the six palm trees?

6. How many flags are there on the island?

Now see if any of your friends and family can do it from memory.

Simply let them study the map for two minutes then cover it up and see how many questions they can answer correctly.

NELSON'S COLUMN

Go dotty with these dot-to-dot challenges.

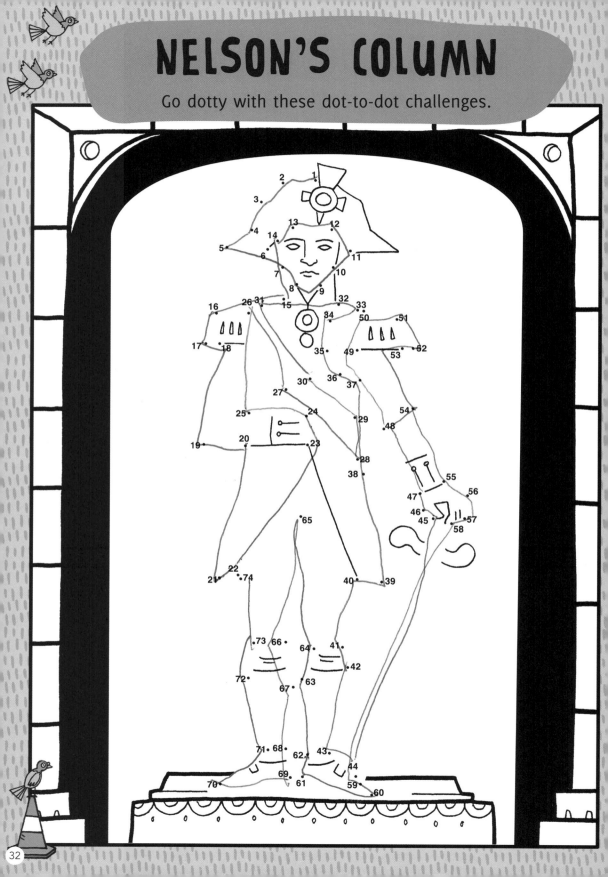

PUZZLE HOTEL

Can you spot seven differences between these two hotel rooms?
Once you've spotted them all, colour the two scenes in.

Follow the instructions to complete these perplexing puzzles.

Look at these room keys.
Which two keys are exactly the same?

Can you find your way through the corridors to the rooftop restaurant?

Which bag belongs to which family member?

123 ...

Spot all the items listed in the box
on the opposite page.

VENICE – ITALY

5 Busts

7 Roman vases

8 Bottles of olive oil

4 Pizzas

4 Venetian masks

12 Gondoliers

8 Ice creams

7 Holdalls

OUT AT SEA

Follow the colour key to reveal the beautiful boats.

Draw and colour all the things you would find on your dream island.

SPOT THE DIFFERENCE

Can you find the 8 differences
between these two scenes?

WATER-SKI

Can you work out which two water-skiers have lost their boats?

SUMMER AT THE THEME PARK

Can you find your way around
the rides at the theme park?

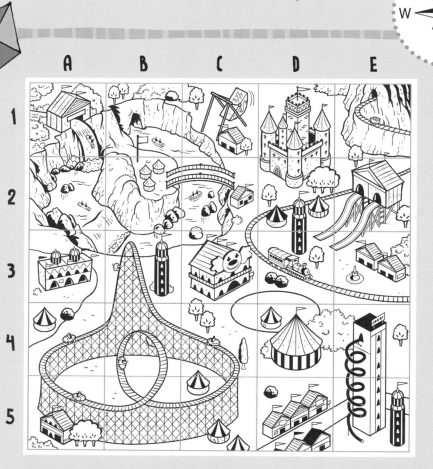

Start at the square indicated by the number and the letter in brackets, then find your way around the park following the directions on the compass below.

Example: The Giant Swing (1C). If you walk 2 South, 2 East, 2 South, 1 West, 1 North you end up at the Big Top (4D).

1. Starting from the Spiral Slide (5E):
   2 North, 2 West, 1 South, 1 East

2. Starting from the Rickety Bridge (2C):
   2 South, 2 West,
   3 North

3. Starting from the Coaster (5A): 2 North, 4 East, 1 North

PUZZLE CITY

The city never sleeps and neither will you
with these puzzles keeping you awake.

CAPITAL CITY CHECKLIST

Match the capital cities to the countries in which they are found.
The first one has been done for you to get you started.

Bangkok — Australia
New Delhi — USA
Beijing — Thailand
Madrid — India
Moscow — Russia
Berlin — China
Paris — France
Washington, DC — Spain
Canberra — Germany

ROUND THE BLOCK

Follow the directions below and see where you would end up.

Turn right out of garage A and take the first right. Turn right again, then take the first left. Take the second right, then turn left and then take the first left.

Which garage do you end up in, B or C?

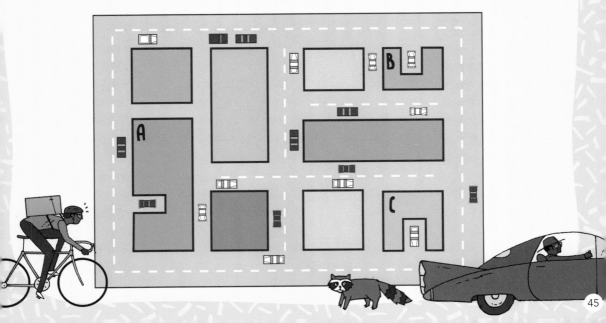

TEEPEE TENTS

Follow the colour key to reveal these quirky tents.

ULTIMATE I-SPY

Keep your eyes peeled to make long,
boring road journeys fly by.

You can play this game with as many people as you
like. When each item on the list below is spotted, write
the initials of the person who spotted it first in the box.

When all the items have been spotted the
spotter who has spotted the most, wins.

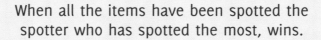

1. A yellow car		16. A horse box	
2. A post box		17. A traffic jam	
3. A tree with no leaves		18. A sports car	
4. A river		19. Someone running	
5. A set of traffic lights		20. A sign for a theme park	
6. An electricity pylon		21. A service station	
7. A red lorry		22. A hot-air balloon	
8. A sheep		23. Graffiti	
9. A cow		24. A child on roller skates	
10. A church		25. A woman in a purple hat	
11. A castle		26. A police car	
12. A flag		27. A broken-down vehicle	
13. A bird of prey		28. A bridge	
14. A tractor		29. A boat (of any kind)	
15. A caravan		30. An aeroplane taking off	

BARMY BALLOONS

Fill the sky with hot-air balloons.

GO WILD

Follow the colour key to bring these wild animals to life.

123 ...

Spot all the items listed in the box on the opposite page.

SYDNEY — AUSTRALIA

- 10 Volleyballs ✓
- 6 Didgeridoos ✓
- 7 Turtles
- 10 Koalas
- 8 Seagulls
- 7 Boomerangs
- 15 Kangaroos
- 7 Meat pies

PEACE PAGODA

Join the dots to reveal a charming pagoda.

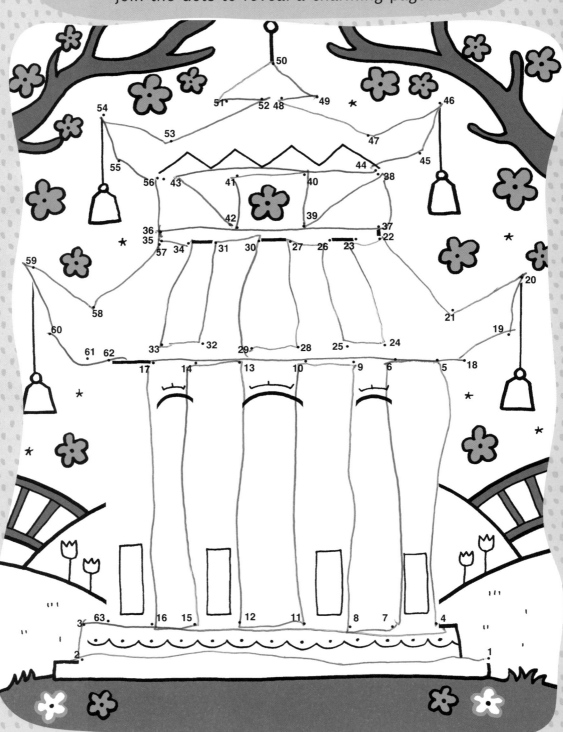

BIRD WATCHERS

Complete the maze to help these bird watchers get closer to the birds.

COLOUR IN THE
GREAT BARRIER REEF

WATER WORLD

Which swimmer will come out of which flume?

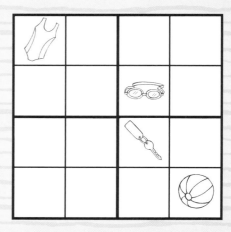

Complete the grid above so that each column, each row, and each of the four larger squares contains only one swimsuit, a beach ball, a locker key and some goggles.

Using only three straight lines, divide the swimming pool into six sections, with one swimmer and one beach ball in each.

Can you spot two identical burgers in this diner?

Can you find a clear path for this girl through the maze to the jacuzzi?

SHELL-TASTIC

Decorate these shells with
eye-catching patterns.

PICTURE POSTCARDS

Join the dots to create postcards to send to friends. Make sure you colour them in.

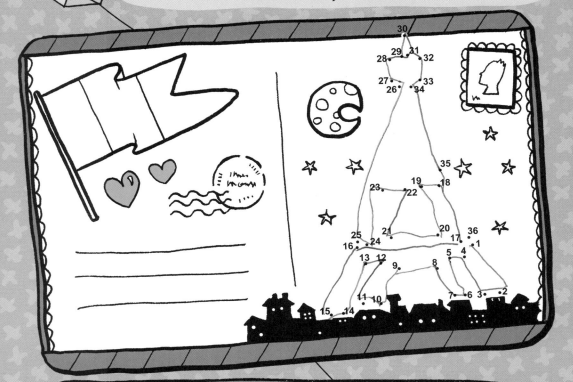

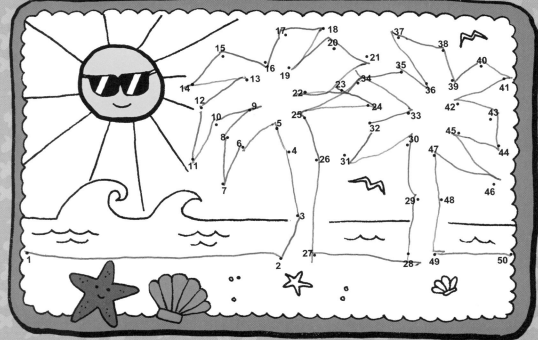

63

WINDOW WATCH

Draw what you saw on your journey.

SUMMER SAFARI

What has the explorer discovered
in the rainforest?

123 ...

Spot all the items listed in the box on the opposite page.

AMSTERDAM – NETHERLANDS

6 Radios

5 Wheels of edam cheese

7 Bunches of purple tulips

5 Red bicycles

4 Paint palettes

36 Ducks

8 Hockey sticks

9 Cups of coffee

GALERIE

PENS AT THE READY

Whether you are on a long car journey or waiting at the airport, be sure to keep a pen and paper handy for games – it will make time fly by.

BOXING MATCH

You will need two players for this game. To begin, draw a grid of dots on your page measuring seven dots by seven dots like the one shown below.

Take it in turns with your opponent to draw a single line that connects two dots. The line must be either horizontal or vertical – no diagonal lines allowed.

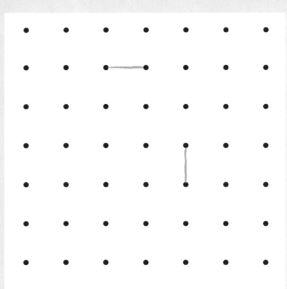

The aim of the game is to complete more boxes than your opponent. When it's your turn, if you find three lines around a box you can finish it with your line and make it yours. Stake your claim by writing the first letter of your name inside. Each time a player completes a box, they can take another turn.

When all the dots have been joined up, count up how many boxes each player has and the person with the most, wins.

TOP TIP: Why not play a really long game with a board measuring 20 dots by 20 dots?

Z	Z	Z	Z	Z	S
Z	Z	Z	Z	Z	S
S	S	Z	Z	Z	Z
S	S	Z	Z	Z	S
S	S	Z	Z	S	S
S	S	Z	Z	S	S

BOX CLEVER

Can you find a place to draw your line that doesn't allow your opponent to complete a square?

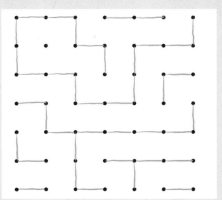

DESERT DOTS

Join up the dots and add some colour to this Egyptian scene.

SHOP 'TIL YOU DROP

Complete the puzzles before the shops close.

Can you spot 11 differences between the two window displays on the opposite page?

Once you have finished, colour it all in.

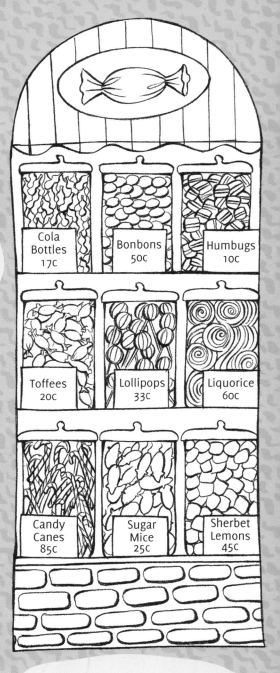

Cola Bottles 17C

Bonbons 50C

Humbugs 10C

Toffees 20C

Lollipops 33C

Liquorice 60C

Candy Canes 85C

Sugar Mice 25C

Sherbet Lemons 45C

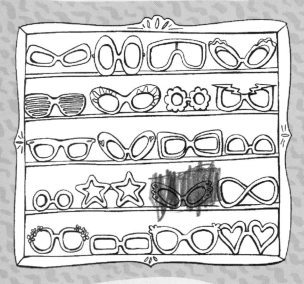

Can you find the sunglasses that match the ones pictured in the magazine above?

You have 300 cents (c) in your purse. If you were going to use all of your money to buy one type of sweet, how many of each type could you buy?

UP, UP AND AWAY

Follow the colour key to bring these hot-air balloons to life.

FISH FOR SUPPER

Add more fish to complete this bait ball.

DESIGN YOUR OWN STAMPS

SEA VOYAGE

Complete the maze to take the diver to the bottom of the sea.

SPOT THE DIFFERENCE

Can you find the 8 differences
between these two scenes?

ROAD TRIP

Have you ever imagined taking a road trip in the car of your dreams? If so, you'll enjoy being behind the wheel on this puzzle adventure.

AMERICAN ADVENTURE

You've decided to take a road trip around America. You're going to make three separate car journeys, and one aeroplane flight. Can you work out which cities you will pass through on each trip described below? Now write down which three cities you will not visit because you don't pass through the squares in which they appear.

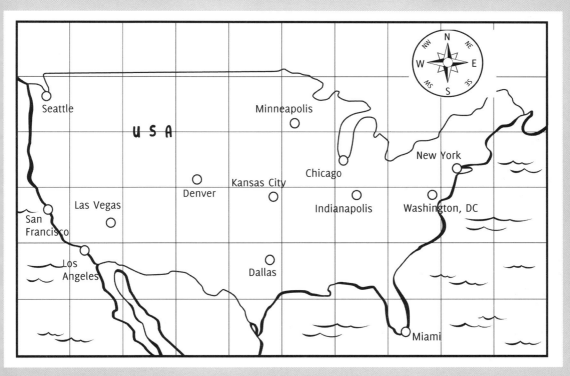

Trip A. From New York, you drive one square west, then three squares south, then one square north, then six squares west.

Trip B. You fly to Seattle. From there you drive five squares east, then one square south, then one square east, then 5 squares west, then one square south.

Trip C. From Las Vegas, you drive one square south, then six squares east, then two squares north and one square east.

IN TOO DEEP

Draw what you think could be lurking in the darkness.

WORLD FACTS QUIZ

Test out your family's knowledge of the world with this fun, fact-filled quiz. Write each player's answers – A, B, C or D – in the scorecard on the opposite page.

1. The Eiffel Tower is a tourist attraction in which city?

A. New York
B. Beijing
C. Paris
D. Rome

2. In which country are you most likely to eat spaghetti?

A. Japan
B. Italy
C. India
D. Nepal

3. Where do kangaroos come from?

A. Singapore
B. Cambodia
C. Canada
D. Australia

4. Where are the pharaohs buried?

A. The Leaning Tower of Pisa, Italy
B. The Pantheon, Greece
C. The Pyramids of Egypt
D. Buckingham Palace, England

5. In which country is the Taj Mahal?

A. France
B. Portugal
C. Italy
D. India

6. Which language do most people speak in Brazil?

A. Portuguese
B. Chinese
C. English
D. French

7. What are the Niagara Falls?

A. Waterfalls
B. Mountains
C. Pyramids
D. Oceans

8. Which of these is an animal-watching holiday in Africa?

A. A hike
B. A cruise
C. A marathon
D. A safari

9. What is the world's favourite ice-cream flavour?

A. Chilli
B. Pineapple
C. Lime
D. Vanilla

10. Which of these islands would you find in the Caribbean Sea?

A. Jamaica
B. Ireland
C. Australia
D. Iceland

11. What kind of money could you spend in India?

    A. Rupee
    B. Whoopee
    C. Loopee
    D. Hoopee

13. In which country do people famously eat snails?

    A. Greenland
    B. Norway
    C. France
    D. Italy

12. Which of these words means 'Hello' in Spanish?

    A. Bonjour
    B. Hola
    C. Howdy
    D. Paella

14. Which country held the Olympics in 2016?

    A. The USA
    B. Great Britain
    C. China
    D. Brazil

Question	Player One	Player Two	Player Three	Player Four
1				
2				
3				
4				
5				
6				
7				
8				
9				
10				
11				
12				
13				
14				
TOTAL SCORE				

SAIL AWAY

Doodle designs on these sails.

MARKET TRADE

Complete the maze to help the traders
collect their goods to sell.

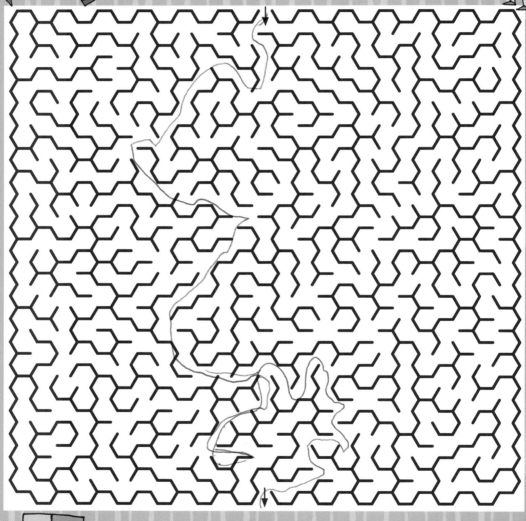

MESSAGE IN A BOTTLE

You are strolling by the sea when all of a sudden you spy a plastic bottle. Then another, and then another. You notice that each bottle contains a rolled up piece of paper ...

1. On the paper inside the first bottle, you find the following cryptic message:

'X L M T I Z G F O Z G R L M H!
B L F   S Z E V   D L M   Z   U I V V
R X V   X I V Z N!'

Need a clue to decode it? Write the alphabet backwards under a normal alphabet and substitute each letter in the message for the letter below it. Can you work out what it says?

2. You look inside the second bottle and find this message:

K I V H V M G   G S V H V
N V H H Z T V H   Z G   Q L V' H
X Z U V   G L   X O Z R N...

Can you work out what it means?

3. The third bottle contains an even stranger-looking message. On the paper you find the grid below and this cryptic message:

'Colour in the squares you need, to show you something you can read.'

Can you crack the code?

2 4 7	A	E	G	E	L	A	R
1 3 6 7	A	S	G	S	O	A	L
2 5	F	K	H	O	E	M	E
1 3 6	F	M	L	A	D	B	E
1 4 5	M	L	E	U	A	M	O
2 3 5 6 7	N	E	F	A	W	M	L
1 3 4 6 7	A	D	A	A	E	A	H

ALL THE ANSWERS

AHOY THERE!
(PAGES 4 AND 5)

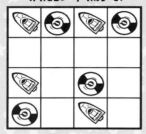

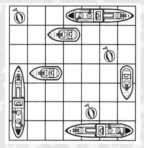

SECRET SAFARI
(PAGE 10)

1. Giraffes, 2. Monkeys, 3. Deer
4. Lion, 5. Zebra, 6. Hippos

FIND THE MISSING NUMBER
(PAGE 11)

Elephant = 1, Tiger = 2,
Rhino = 3, Lion = 4, ? = 10

PICTURE PUZZLER
(PAGES 16 AND 17)

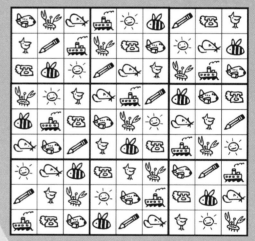

GONE FISHING
(PAGE 22)

TREASURE HUNT
(PAGE 23)

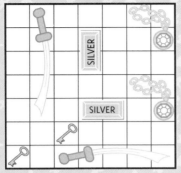

MAP MAYHEM
(PAGE 30)

5A is a swimming pool.
4E is a café.
1F is a school.
3B is a theme park.
6D is a hospital.
3G is a cinema.

ISLAND DISCOVERY
(PAGE 31)

1. 12
2. 5
3. West
4. A lighthouse
5. A swimming pool
6. 6

SPOT THE DIFFERENCE
(PAGE 26)

PUZZLE HOTEL
(PAGES 34 AND 35)

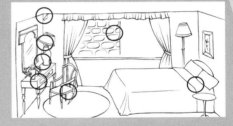

Room keys C and L
are identical.

Person 1 has bag A.
Person 2 has bag C.
Person 3 has bag D.
Person 4 has bag B.

THINGS THAT GO
(PAGE 27)

Wheels C and G, B and D, E
and I, and A and F are the
same. Wheel H is unique.

Kit B contains all the bits
to build the plane.

The pieces match the
following squares:
H8, B4 and J2.

123 ... VENICE, ITALY
(PAGES 36 AND 37)

SPOT THE DIFFERENCE
(PAGE 42)

WATER-SKI
(PAGE 43)

Skiers A and C have lost their boats.

SUMMER AT THE THEME PARK
(PAGE 44)

1. The Big Top (4D)
2. Thunder River (1A)
3. The Slip and Slide (2E)

PUZZLE CITY
(PAGE 45)

CAPITAL CITY CHECKLIST:
Bangkok = Thailand
New Delhi = India
Beijing = China
Madrid = Spain

Moscow = Russia
Berlin = Germany
Paris = France
Washington, DC = USA
Canberra = Australia

ROUND THE BLOCK:
You would end up in garage C.

123 ... SYDNEY, AUSTRALIA
(PAGES 52 AND 53)

BIRD WATCHERS
(PAGE 55)

WATER WORLD
(PAGES 58 AND 59)

Swimmer A reaches flume 1.   Swimmer C reaches flume 3.
Swimmer B reaches flume 2.   Swimmer D reaches flume 4.

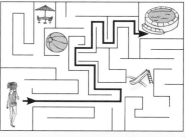

123 ... AMSTERDAM, THE NETHERLANDS
(PAGES 66 AND 67)

SHOP 'TIL YOU DROP
(PAGES 72 AND 73)

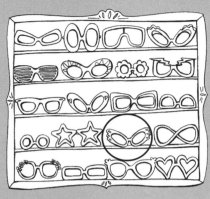

In the sweet shop you could buy:

17 cola bottles with 11c left over,

6 bonbons, 30 humbugs, 15 toffees,
9 lollipops with 3c left over,

5 liquorices, 3 candy canes with 45c
left over,

12 sugar mice, 6 sherbet lemons
with 30c left over.

SEA VOYAGE
(PAGE 79)

SPOT THE DIFFERENCE
(PAGE 80)

ROAD TRIP
(PAGE 81)

Trip A. New York, Washington, DC, Miami, Dallas, Los Angeles.

Trip B. Seattle, Minneapolis, Chicago, Denver, Las Vegas.

Trip C. Las Vegas, Los Angeles, Dallas, Washington, DC, New York.

You have not visited San Francisco, Kansas City or Indianapolis.

MARKET TRADE
(PAGE 88)

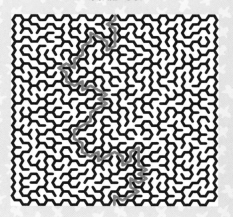

WORLD FACTS QUIZ
(PAGES 84 AND 85)

1. C	8. D
2. B	9. D
3. D	10. A
4. C	11. A
5. D	12. B
6. A	13. C
7. A	14. D

MESSAGE IN A BOTTLE
(PAGE 89)

1. Message reads: 'Congratulations! You have won a free ice cream!'

2. The alphabet is spelt out backwards again. The decoded message spells out: 'Present these messages at Joe's Café to claim...'

3. Colour in the squares matching the numbers by each row. The letters left spell out: 'A glass of home-made lemonade'.